Alice
and
Greta

Dedicated to: Eileen, Sara, Caroline,
Julia, Nick and Cliff—
with much love, and thanks for listening!
— S.J.S.

For S.R.B.
with love and gratitude
— C.M.

ISBN 0-590-41722-3

Text copyright © 1997 by Steven J. Simmons.
Illustrations copyright © 1997 by Cyd Moore.
All rights reserved.
Published by Scholastic Inc., 555 Broadway, New York, NY 10012,
by arrangement with Charlesbridge Publishing.

12 11 10   2 3/0

Printed in the U.S.A.   14

First Scholastic printing, October 1998

The display type and text type were set in Leawood.

Alice and Greta

A TALE OF
TWO WITCHES

Steven J. Simmons
Illustrated by Cyd Moore

SCHOLASTIC INC.
New York Toronto London Auckland Sydney

Welcome!

Once, a long time ago, two witches lived on top of a mountain. Although they both looked out at the same view, they saw things differently.

KEEP AWAY!

Alice's outlook, like her clothes, was always rosy.

Greta, on the other hand, was always on the lookout for trouble. She dressed in poison green—a color she liked to think was as putrid as her personality.

Oh, how different Alice and Greta were!

Alice and Greta had known each other ever since they were little witches at Miss Mildred Mildew's School of Magic. There they had learned the same spells,

. . . the same curses,

Thanks for the warts, Alice!

GRRREETAAAA!

. . . the same chants,

Gnats Knees, dragon fleas, donkey breath, spider sneeze...

. . . and the same brews.

They just used their magic differently.

Whereas Alice's spells were simply enchanting . . .

. . . Greta's were deviously diabolical.

The Brewmerang Principle:
Whatever you chant,
Whatever you brew,
Sooner or later
Comes back to you!

The Brewmerang Principle

Greta never did her homework and often didn't listen in class. She was misbehaving as usual the day the class learned the most important lesson of all.

Time passed and before long, it was graduation day.
Alice and Greta flew off into the world to weave their spells
and work their witchery.

One day, Alice was flying high above the seashore when she spotted a sailboat stranded on a sandbar. She waved her wand in circles high above her head and whispered:

Come now, Moon, and turn the tide.
Take this family for a ride!

A huge wave rushed toward the boat and lifted it safely off the sandbar. The family waved their thanks.

On the other side of the world, Greta was using the same spell—just a little differently. She saw some children building a sand castle on a beach. They had worked for hours on the towers, tunnels, and moat.

Just as they finished, Greta waved her wand in circles high above her head and whispered:

Come now, Moon, and turn the tide.
Take this castle for a ride!

An enormous wave crashed high on the beach,
sweeping the castle into the sea.

"Ah, ha-ha!" Greta cackled. Then she disappeared
into a cloud as the children ran crying to their mothers.

Meanwhile, Alice had come upon
a small boy in a field calling for
his lost puppy. Alice knew what
to do. She waved her wand and
chanted:

Alcazam, alcazeer!
Puppy dog, reappear.

A sheepdog pup bounded out of the woods and into the grateful boy's arms. Alice smiled and was on her way.

At that moment, Greta was busy being a bad sport. She had passed a school soccer team playing for the league championship. As one girl was about to kick a goal, Greta waved her wand and chanted:

Alcazam, alcazeer!
Soccer balls, disappear!

Not only the girl's ball, but every ball on the field disappeared.

The puzzled players searched until dark, but they couldn't find a single ball to finish the game. Everyone went home, perplexed and disappointed. Greta snickered and flew home to her cave, delighted with her dirty work.

The next day, Greta was sipping her morning cup of pond slime. She was bored. It was time to stir up trouble, but where? She tossed a few things into the cauldron. When the smoke cleared, she peered into the brew and muttered:

Time to brew, time to bubble,
Time to stir up nasty trouble!

In the boiling potion she saw a school playground and children happily playing. Greta jumped on her broom and flew off in search of the school.

Within minutes, she arrived at the same scene that had appeared in her cauldron. Rubbing her hands with delight, Greta said, "The children are so sweet. But I can make them even sweeter . . ." She waved her wand at the fluffy clouds overhead and cackled:

Icky, yicky, gloppy gloop,
Clouds, spill down my sticky soup!

With a crash and a flash, the fluffy clouds overhead rained down millions of melting marshmallows onto the children. At first the children were delighted. But as soon as they realized they were stuck in the gooey, sticky marshmallow mess, they called for help. Greta just laughed and laughed.

Alice heard their cries and appeared from behind a cloud. But before she could lift a wand to help, Greta spotted her. "Oh no you don't!" she yelled, and pointed her wand at Alice.

Icky, sticky, gloppy goo,
Another sweetie for the stew!

A million more marshmallows fell on Alice. Before she knew it, she and her broomstick were pulled to the ground and stuck fast in an icky, sticky mess. She was helpless, unable to lift her magic wand.

Alice struggled, desperate to think of what to do.
Then she remembered something she had learned in
school. She looked hard at Greta and said these words:

Whatever you chant, whatever you brew,
Sooner or later, comes back to you!"

Nothing happened. So Alice added a little spell of
her own.

Make it sooner, not too late.
Help me now, I just can't wait!

With that, the marshmallows lifted
off Alice and the children and landed—
THWAP!—on top of Greta.

The children crowded around Alice
and cheered!

To this day, Alice lives in her cave on the hill, where the view just keeps getting better and better.

And for now, Greta is stuck learning something she should have learned long ago.